AVAILABLE NOW
from Lerner Publishing Services!

The *On the Hardwood* series:

Atlanta Hawks	Los Angeles Lakers
Boston Celtics	Memphis Grizzlies
Brooklyn Nets	Miami Heat
Chicago Bulls	Minnesota Timberwolves
Cleveland Cavaliers	New York Knicks
Dallas Mavericks	Oklahoma City Thunder
Denver Nuggets	Phoenix Suns
Detroit Pistons	Philadelphia 76ers
Golden State Warriors	Portland Trail Blazers
Houston Rockets	San Antonio Spurs
Indiana Pacers	Utah Jazz
Los Angeles Clippers	Washington Wizards

Hoop City *Long Shot*

Basketball fans: don't miss these hoops books from MVP's wing-man, Scobre Educational.

These titles, and many others, are available at www.scobre.com.

To Order • www.lernerbooks.com • 800-328-4929 • fax 800-332-1132

ON THE HARDWOOD

ATLANTA HAWKS

ZACH WYNER

J. Lupton Simpson Middle School
Loudoun County Public Schools

On the Hardwood: Atlanta Hawks

Copyright © 2014
by Zach Wyner

All rights reserved.

Printed in the United States of America.

No part of this book may be reproduced in any manner whatsoever without written permission, except in the case of brief quotations embodied in critical articles and reviews.

MVP Books
2255 Calle Clara
La Jolla, CA 92037

MVP Books is an imprint of Scobre Educational, a division of Book Buddy Digital Media, Inc.,
42982 Osgood Road, Fremont, CA 94539

MVP Books publications may be purchased for
educational, business, or sales promotional use.

Cover and layout design by Jana Ramsay
Copyedited by Susan Sylvia
Photos by Getty Images

ISBN: 978-1-61570-898-7 (Library Binding)
ISBN: 978-1-61570-897-0 (Soft Cover)

The NBA and individual NBA member team identifications are trademarks, copyrighted designs, and/or other forms of intellectual property that are the exclusive property of NBA Properties, Inc. and the respective NBA member teams and may not be used, in whole or in part, without the prior written consent of NBA Properties, Inc.

© 2014 NBA Properties, Inc.

All rights reserved.

TABLE OF CONTENTS

Chapter 1	Flying South	6
Chapter 2	Wheeling and Dealing	14
Chapter 3	The Human Highlight Film	22
Chapter 4	The Duel and The Gentle Giant	32
Chapter 5	Soaring into the Future	40

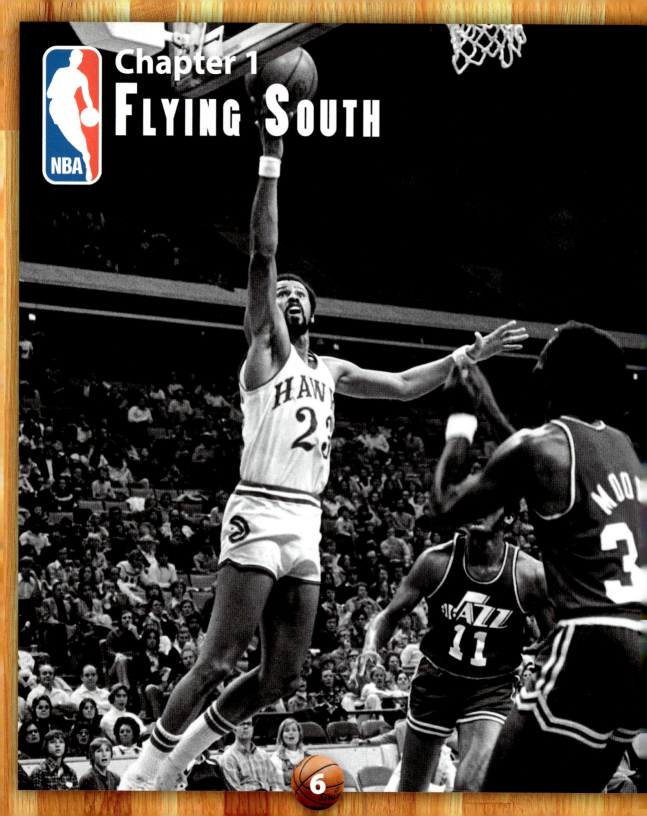

Chapter 1
Flying South

The 1958 NBA Finals was a battle between two of the greatest big men in the history of the game. Bill Russell of the Boston Celtics was the reigning champion. In fact, including back-to-back NCAA titles won at the University of San Francisco, Russell had finished the basketball season with a championship trophy for three straight years. Bob Petit of the St. Louis Hawks had already had his number retired by Louisiana State University (LSU) and won two 1956 NBA MVPs—All Star Game and regular season. Both men were terrors on the boards, but Russell's legacy is as one of the game's great defenders, while Petit's career scoring average of 26.4 points per game is still the seventh highest in league history. In the 1958 Finals, Bob Petit put his team on his back and did something no team was able to do for the next eight years–beat Boston. His 50 points in Game 6 set a record for most points in a Finals game and he guided the Hawks to

He's #1
In 1956, Bob Petit won the first ever NBA MVP Award.

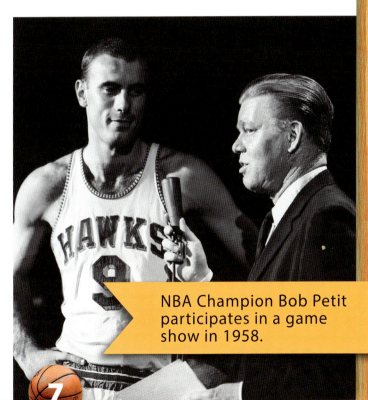

NBA Champion Bob Petit participates in a game show in 1958.

Hall of Famer Bill Russell shoots over Hall of Famer Bob Petit.

an NBA Championship.

The Hawks franchise (first known at the "Bisons" and later as the "Blackhawks") moved a lot in their early years. While the team originated in Buffalo, New York, they soon journeyed to an area called the Tri-Cities that borders Illinois and Iowa. From there, they moved to Milwaukee, Wisconsin, where they changed their name to "Hawks" and drafted Bob Petit, a future Hall of Famer and one of the NBA's 50 Greatest Players. However, even with the acquisition of Petit, the Hawks did not draw a large enough crowd to sustain the team. Eventually, they landed in St. Louis, Missouri, where they won a championship and appeared to settle into their Midwest digs. During their 13 seasons in St. Louis, the Hawks made the playoffs 12 times, advancing all the way to the Finals in 1957 and 1958, and again in 1960 and 1961. Unfortunately, they kept running into Boston. While the Hawks emerged victorious in 1958, the Celtics prevented them from winning multiple titles.

By the time 1965 rolled around,

the Hawks had proven themselves to be one of the NBA's most consistent teams. However, with the retirement of Bob Petit and the city's refusal to build a new arena, their days in St. Louis were numbered. In 1968, the team was sold and moved to Atlanta, Georgia, the first southern state to host an NBA franchise. The move came during a tumultuous time in the history of the region.

In the 1960s, Atlanta was a place of social and political unrest. Home to historically black colleges such as Morehouse, Spelman, and Clark University, Atlanta was, and remains, a foundation of black scholarship. However, the existence of African American universities did not make Atlanta a city of tolerance

Unimaginable Loss
In 1968, Dr. Martin Luther King, Jr. and Senator Robert Kennedy were both assassinated.

and opportunity. In 1968, the South had only recently been integrated. Years of protest, of people sacrificing their freedom and sometimes their lives to make the United States a land of equal opportunity, had led to the Civil Rights Act of 1964 and the end of the Jim Crow laws

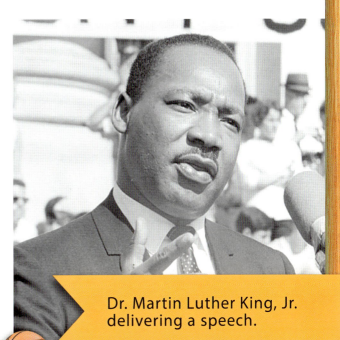

Dr. Martin Luther King, Jr. delivering a speech.

Getting Out The Vote
The Atlanta Negro Voters League, started in 1949, helped elect Ivan Allen, Jr., an MLK supporter, as the city's mayor.

that required segregation. But the end of racist laws did not mean the end of racism. In 1968, the year in which Martin Luther King, Jr. was assassinated, Georgia was still undergoing major changes. Whites and blacks had only been eating at the same lunch counters for a few years, and public schools had only recently been integrated. However, Atlanta's elected leadership believed in Martin Luther King, Jr.'s attempts to end segregation. They were not about to let his ideas die.

Through sit-ins and marches, speeches and elections, the people of Atlanta had shown that they were serious about putting an end to racism in their city. Mindful of the police brutality that had occurred in southern cities that resisted a peaceful transition to equal rights, Atlanta's leaders listened to the people. Although still segregated, Atlanta publicly embraced diversity. The city developed mass transit systems and welcomed businesses and sports franchises. The city wanted to show the country that they were serious about change. In 1966, they premiered two new sports franchises for all their residents to get behind: the Atlanta Braves and the Atlanta Falcons. Two years later, the Atlanta Hawks joined the club.

When the Hawks migrated south, they did so with the promise of moving into a brand new facility. However, with the state-of-the-art Omni Center still under construction, the Hawks were treated to their first taste of southern hospitality. For four years they played their home games at Georgia Tech University's War Memorial Coliseum. Led by four-time All Star "Sweet" Lou Hudson, they won the Western Division title in 1970. The next year, Sweet Lou was joined by "Pistol" Pete Maravich, a flashy guard out of LSU whose arrival in the NBA generated quite a buzz.

Sweet Lou and Pistol Pete were an unlikely match. The Pistol had earned his nickname and fame for his run-and-gun style of play. He would launch shots from anywhere on the court and his behind-the-back passes and circus-like ball-handling skills awed basketball fans everywhere he played. He entered the NBA on the heels of an incredible run at LSU, where he averaged 44.2 points per game over a four-year span. When asked if his flashy style and shot selection was appropriate at the professional level, Pistol Pete said, "There's nothing that says you can't win and be entertaining."

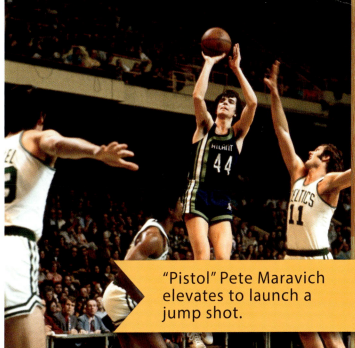

"Pistol" Pete Maravich elevates to launch a jump shot.

"Sweet" Lou Hudson poses for a portrait after the Hawks move to Atlanta.

gave him. His career shooting percentage of 49% (extremely high for a jump shooter) illustrates how selective he was.

Despite their differences in style, Sweet Lou and Pistol Pete played quite well together. In fact, during Pistol Pete's rookie season, Sweet Lou averaged a career high in points. Unfortunately, the Hawks didn't have the depth to put together a winning record. Attendance was up, but the Hawks wanted to do more than sell tickets... they wanted to win games.

In contrast to Pistol Pete, Sweet Lou's game was conservative. While he had one of the best jump shots in the league, he wasn't the type of player to fire away at any old time. Sweet Lou played within the offense, and took the shots that the defense

Sweet Lou and Pistol Pete enjoyed their best year together during the 1972-73 season. In the Hawks' first season playing in the Omni Center, the two guards combined to average over 53 points, 10 assists, and 10 rebounds per game. Although the Hawks were unable to advance past the Eastern Conference Semifinals, they gained national attention. However, the following year, despite Pistol Pete's increased scoring and assists, the Hawks fell below .500 and missed the playoffs. The time had come to make a change. Eager to bring Pistol Pete back to Louisiana, the New Orleans Jazz offered two players and four draft picks. The Hawks accepted the offer and set their sights on the 1975 NBA Draft.

Pete Maravich pushes the ball up the floor against the Boston Celtics.

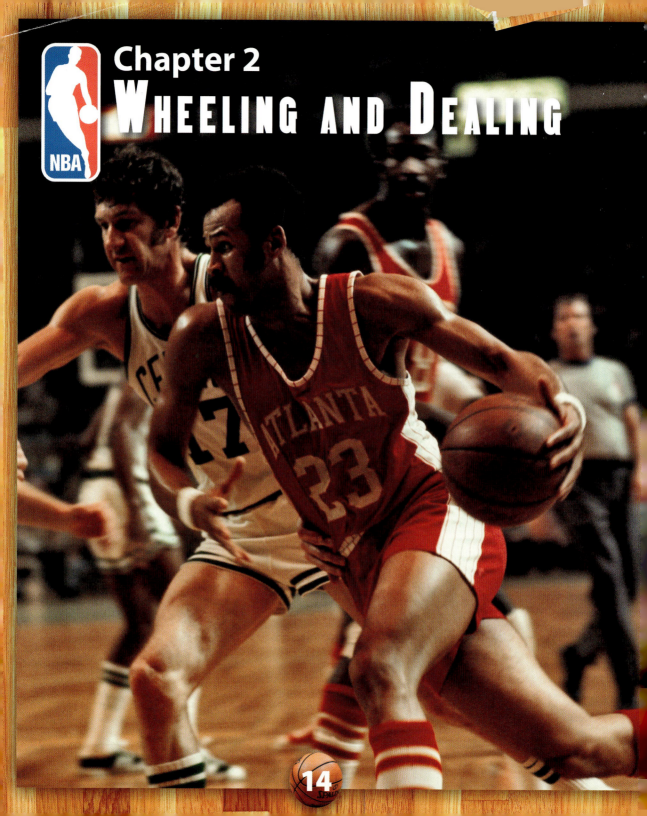

The word "rebuilding" provokes groans from fans everywhere. While fans know that rebuilding can be a necessary step on the path to winning, it's hard to enter into a season with low expectations. Instead of hoping for a spot in the playoffs or a run at the title, they try to root for small victories. They hope for improvements in team chemistry. They hope that increased playing time will grow a young player's confidence. They hope that a coach will put a system into place that is exciting to watch and suits the strengths of the team's best players. And they hope that draft picks show that they can compete at the professional level. But before those draft picks try to up their game, there is one other thing that they hope for—that drafted players sign with the team that drafted them.

The 1975 NBA Draft delivered a devastating blow to the Hawks and their fans. Coming off a rough first

> **Models of Consistency**
> Between 1962 and 1973, the Hawks never missed the postseason, qualifying for the playoffs 11 straight times.

A former #1 draft pick, Bellamy had his best season as a Hawk in 1971-72, averaging 19 points and 13 rebounds.

season without Pistol Pete, the team comforted itself in the knowledge that they had the 1st and 3rd picks in the draft. With the play of Sweet Lou and Hawks' center Walt Bellamy on the decline, the Hawks needed youth and talent. The 1st and 3rd picks in the draft were certain to deliver. Imagine if the Cleveland Cavaliers had been able to draft LeBron James and Carmelo Anthony in 2003, or if the Los Angeles Clippers had been able to draft Blake Griffin and James Harden in 2009. With the 1st and 3rd selections in the 1975 NBA Draft, the Atlanta Hawks selected David Thompson of North Carolina State and Marvin Webster of Morgan State. The future looked bright. David Thompson was a 6'4" guard who could light things up from outside and rain down thunderous dunks on the heads of opponents. Nicknamed the "Human Eraser" for his shot-blocking abilities, 7'1" Marvin Webster averaged eight blocks per game during his final college season. Hawks' management and fans imagined their team flying into the playoffs in no time.

Sadly, a Webster/Thompson

David Thompson was nicknamed "Skywalker" because of his 44" vertical leap.

"Doctor" Hubie Brown coached the Hawks from 1976 to 1981.

duo was not meant to be. The Hawks had overlooked one minor roadblock in the draft—the American Basketball Association (ABA). A smaller professional basketball league that was formed in 1967, the ABA was getting more attention by the mid-1970s. Their marquee team—the New York Nets—featured a player by the name of Julius "Dr. J" Erving who was creating more excitement than any basketball player on the planet. Noting the growth of the ABA and the amount of money they could earn playing there, Thompson and Webster both chose to sign on with the ABA's Denver Nuggets. The Hawks had traded away Pistol Pete Maravich for a first-round draft pick and now they had virtually nothing to show for it.

It took some time, but by 1979

Come Together
The ABA and the NBA merged in 1977 when four teams from the ABA (Spurs, Nuggets, Pacers, and Nets) joined the National Basketball Association.

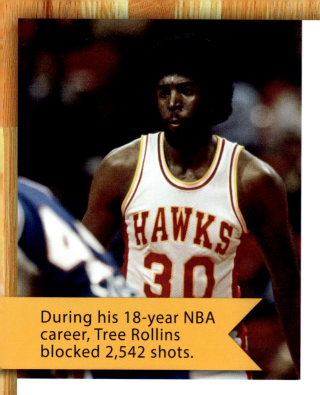

During his 18-year NBA career, Tree Rollins blocked 2,542 shots.

the Hawks began clawing their way back to respectability. The team had been sold to billionaire media big shot, Ted Turner, and his first act of business was hiring the now-legendary "Doctor" Hubie Brown as head coach. The Hawks then picked up 7'1" center Wayne "Tree" Rollins

3's A Charm
Dominique Wilkins was selected third in the 1982 NBA Draft behind James Worthy and Terry Cummings.

and guard Eddie Johnson. In 1980, Hubie Brown coached the Hawks to a Central Division title. It was the team's first division title since 1970, and their first 50-win season since 1967-68. But in the 1980-81 season, the Hawks collapsed, finishing 20 games under .500. Hubie Brown's stint as head coach ended after five seasons, and the Hawks once again looked to the draft for help.

The 1982 NBA Draft was as good to the Hawks as the 1975 draft had been painful. But it wasn't the Hawks' draft pick that was to change the face of Atlanta basketball for the next 12 years. Dominique Wilkins, the star forward for the University of Georgia was first drafted by the Utah Jazz. Fortunately for Hawks fans, the Jazz were having cash flow problems and could not afford to sign the man who would soon be known nationwide as the "Human Highlight Film," or more simply as "Nique." In one of the most lopsided trades in the history of the NBA, the Atlanta Hawks sent John Drew, Freeman Williams, and cash to Utah for Dominique.

The son of a military man, Dominique Wilkins was born in Paris, France, while his father was stationed there. When they returned to the United States, the family settled in Baltimore, Maryland, where Dominique earned a reputation playing pick-up ball on the tough playgrounds at Patterson Park and Sparrows Point. The prevailing opinion held by the streetballers was that Dominique would go pro, but Dominique was just a teenager, not even old enough to drive a car. He knew he could play, but the talk about him playing in the NBA sounded farfetched.

Before his tenth-grade year, Dominique visited his grandmother in Washington, North Carolina. It was there that Washington High School basketball coach Dave Smith saw him play. Having seen Dominique

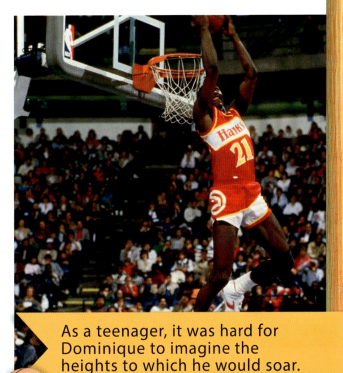

As a teenager, it was hard for Dominique to imagine the heights to which he would soar.

in action, Smith pleaded with Dominique to stay in the basketball-rich area, a mere 100 miles from the city of Raleigh and North Carolina State. Smith's sales pitch worked; Dominique and family packed their bags and headed south.

In his two years at Washington High School, Dominique Wilkins averaged 29 points and 16 rebounds per game. He led his school to back-to-back state championships and became one of the top college recruits in the country. At 6'8", 230 pounds, and with an incredible vertical leap of 47 inches, just about every coach in the country was ready to give their right arm to bring the young star to their team. In the end, it was the University of Georgia, a school with a dominant football team and very little basketball tradition, that Dominique chose to attend. Years later, Norm Sloan (who had been head basketball coach at North Carolina State) said, "I'll certainly never get over losing him." Among other compliments, Sloan called Dominique "the best offensive rebounder in the history of the college game."

Dominique at the University of Georgia, fittingly posed above the rim.

Most great offensive rebounders are big men who use their size and strength to box other players out and move into good rebounding position. Dominique was different. A high-flier with an uncanny knack for reading where the ball was going to bounce, Dominique was what you might call a "swooper." He preferred to stay 12 to 15 feet from the basket and then fall from the ceiling, snatching the ball off the outstretched fingertips of the centers and power forwards. When questioned about his offensive rebounding ability, Dominique said, "I concentrate on reading where shots are likely to come off… And I've worked very hard at different ways to spin off guys outside.

Crashing the Boards
Over the course of his 15-year NBA career, Dominique averaged 2.7 offensive rebounds per game.

I know I want to lay back a little, then just explode up there."

In 1982, Dominique put on a Hawks uniform and exploded onto the NBA scene.

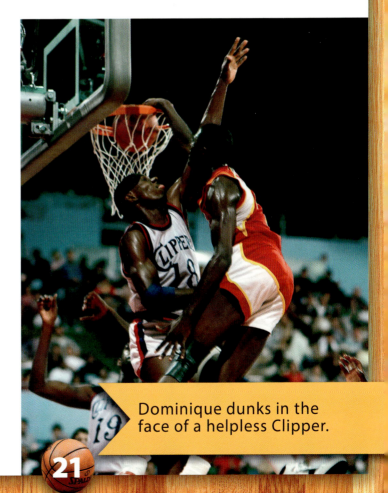

Dominique dunks in the face of a helpless Clipper.

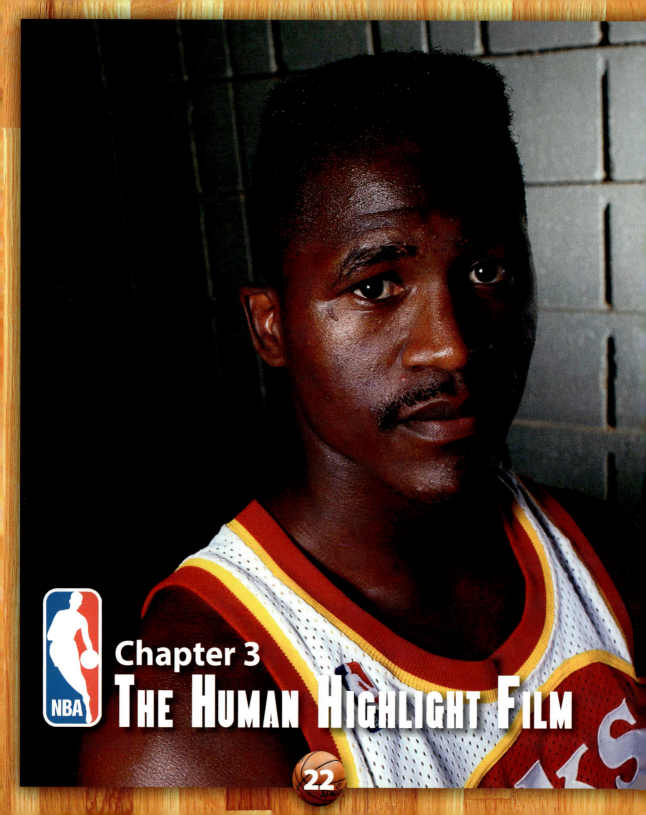

Chapter 3
The Human Highlight Film

Throughout the 1970s, stars like "Sweet" Lou Hudson and "Hammerin'" Hank Aaron led Atlanta-based teams to victory. Both men were ideal teammates, modest and hardworking. But while they were recognized for their greatness and their consistency, fans didn't go crazy for them the way they had for "Pistol" Pete Maravich. "Pistol" Pete played with flare and style—a style whose origins were rooted in streetball and the ABA. As a member of the Hawks, he sparked an interest in the team that simply had not existed before his arrival. In the years following his departure, attendance at home games dwindled. Fans longed to cheer for an athlete who played with

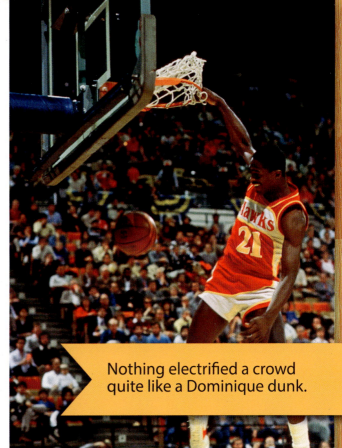

Nothing electrified a crowd quite like a Dominique dunk.

that same exuberance, an athlete who could electrify a crowd and send them home buzzing. Dominique Wilkins was that player.

Not only did Dominique play the game with extraordinary skill, he played with ferocity. The atmosphere generated by the "Human Highlight

Film" was exhilarating. Nique's dunks had become the stuff of legend at the University of Georgia. When he landed in the NBA, his legend spread to every corner of the nation.

When Dominique embarked on his NBA career, a new television network called ESPN had been airing an increasingly popular sports highlight show called "SportsCenter." By watching SportsCenter, basketball fans were no longer limited to three minutes of news coverage on their local team, they were now treated to highlights of teams and players from all over the country. As a result, basketball fans from New York to Los Angeles got a steady dose of Dominique's dunks.

However, back home in Atlanta, Dominique was intent on doing more than making SportsCenter's top 10 plays. Along with management and new coach Mike Fratello, Dominique worked tirelessly to transform the Hawks into a winning team.

Despite his big scoring numbers and individual accolades, two of 'Nique's first three seasons with the Hawks ended with more losses

Mike Fratello coached the Hawks to the playoffs five times in seven years.

than wins. In 1985, 'Nique averaged 27.4 points, 6.9 rebounds, and beat rookie Michael Jordan to win the Slam Dunk Contest; but the Hawks fell to 34-48 and missed the playoffs. Then came 1986. With a roster that now included Kevin Willis, Cliff Livingston, Doc Rivers, and Anthony "Spud" Webb, the Hawks went 35-17 down the stretch and posted their first 50-win season in years.

Led by Dominique Wilkins' league-leading 30.3 points per game, the 1986 Hawks stormed into the playoffs. They quickly dispatched of Isiah Thomas' Detroit Pistons, winning their first playoff series since 1979. Unfortunately, they had little time to celebrate the achievement. Waiting for them in the Eastern Conference Semifinals was Larry Bird's Boston Celtics. The Celtics beat the Hawks four games to one and went on to win the NBA title. But they had not managed to slow down Dominique. The "Human Highlight Film" went toe to toe

Standing Tall
In 1986, 5'7" Spud Webb became the shortest player ever to win the Slam Dunk Contest.

Spud Webb throws down the jam en route to the slam dunk title.

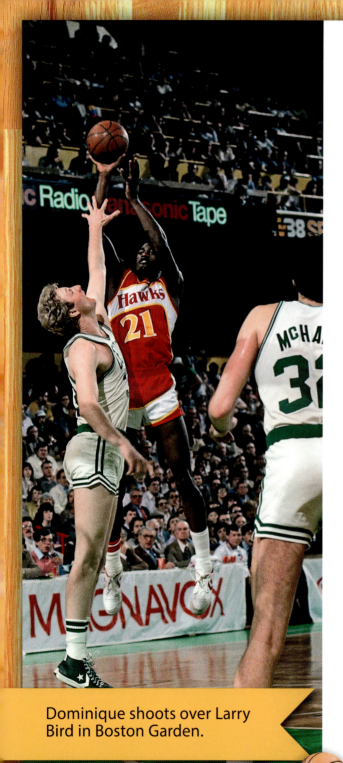

Dominique shoots over Larry Bird in Boston Garden.

with NBA MVP Larry Bird. After struggling in the first two games, Dominique exploded in Games 3 and 4, proving that he was a force to be reckoned with. Although Bird's Celtics won the series, 1986 would not be Dominique's last shot at Larry "Legend".

The 1986-87 season saw the Hawks rise to the top of their division, but their ascent to dominance was not made alone. They had narrowed the gap between themselves and the world champion Boston Celtics, but Isiah Thomas' Detroit Pistons and Michael Jordan's Chicago Bulls were on the rise as well. By April of 1987, the Hawks had won the Central Division title with a franchise-record 57 wins. But in the playoffs, they were derailed by the

"Bad Boys" from Detroit. The disappointing loss would force Dominique to wait another year for his rematch with Larry Bird, and another year for the chance to prove that he was one of the premiere small forwards in the NBA.

While the Hawks slipped a little in the 1987-88 season, losing six of their final nine games, and finishing in a second place tie with Chicago, they were no less confident come playoff time. They beat a tough Milwaukee Bucks team and prepared for the rematch they'd been dreaming of for two years—a seven-game showdown with the Boston Celtics. The Hawks didn't care that the Celtics had finished first in the Eastern Conference. They truly believed that their time had come. Scoring 30.7 points per game while shooting 46% from the field, Dominique had become an unstoppable force. The three-time All-Star was ready for the big stage, eager to lead the city of

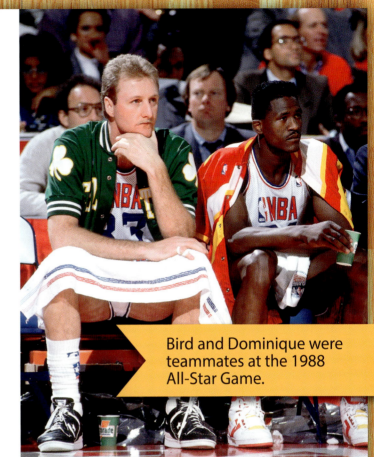

Bird and Dominique were teammates at the 1988 All-Star Game.

> **Deep Hole**
> In NBA playoff history, teams trailing 0-2 in a seven-game series have only come back to win 15 times.

Atlanta where they'd never before gone—the Eastern Conference Finals.

The Celtics won the first two games of the series in convincing fashion. The Hall of Fame trio of Bird, McHale, and Parish was virtually unstoppable, and neither Dominique nor his teammates performed anywhere near well enough to win a game in the Boston Garden. When Kevin Willis and 'Nique led the Hawks in a blowout win in Game 3, experts shrugged. The Celtics hadn't put up much of a fight. If the Hawks were going to win this series, they'd have to win games where the Celtics played well. In Games 4 and 5, the Hawks did just that.

In Game 4, Dominique scored 40 points and Doc Rivers' 15 first-half assists (he finished the game with 22) tied an NBA record. The teams went back to Boston with the series tied. The third quarter of Game 5 ended

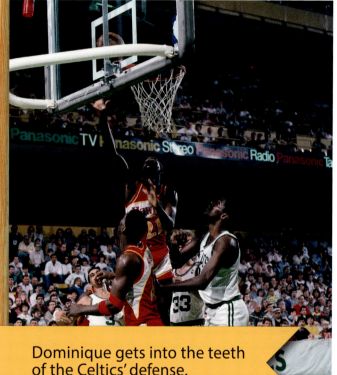

Dominique gets into the teeth of the Celtics' defense.

with the Hawks trailing 77-69. The game appeared to be over. The Celtics rarely lost a Game 5 at home, and with an eight-point lead, this pattern seemed destined to repeat itself. But unwilling to go down without a fight, the Hawks took the floor with incredible aggression. They drove to the basket, and pounded the ball inside. By the end of the quarter, they had made 10 of 15 field goals, 22 free throws, and scored an incredible 43 points on the Celtics' home floor. The Hawks won the game 112-104 and headed back to Atlanta with a chance to close out the series.

When asked about the crowd for Game 6, Hawks radio announcer

Key Reserves
The Hawks' bench contributed to the Game 5 win, outscoring Boston's reserves 30-7.

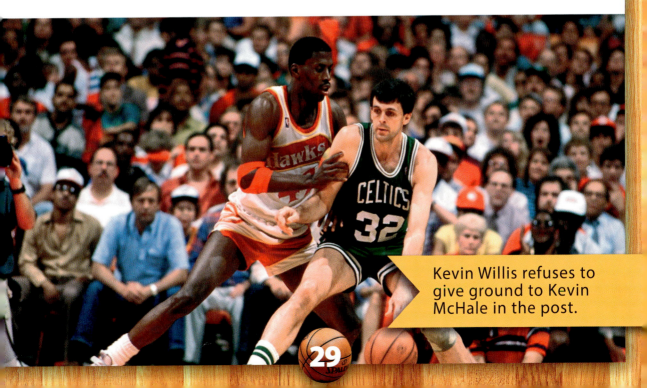

Kevin Willis refuses to give ground to Kevin McHale in the post.

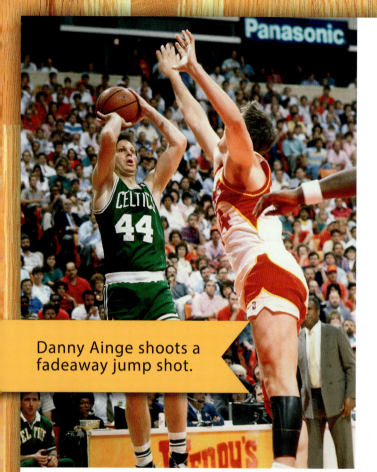

Danny Ainge shoots a fadeaway jump shot.

knew exactly what needed to happen that night. Their team had won three straight, but this was no time for relaxing. They needed to finish off the Celtics and avoid a Game 7 in the Boston Garden.

Despite huge games from Wilkins and Rivers, Danny Ainge's 22 points and 14 assists led the Celtics to a two-point victory. If the Hawks were going to get past the Celtics and into the third round, they'd have to win one more on the road. Years later, still pained by the Game 6 loss, Doc Rivers said, "We had a golden opportunity… After we lost, I remember landing in Boston and this old lady, I bet she was 80 years old, looks at me at the airport… and

Steve Holman said, "The Omni was as raucous as it had ever been. People were hanging from the rafters right from the start, all night." Hawks fans

Memorable Reception
Doc Rivers said about Atlanta's home crowd for Game 6, "I had never seen Atlanta like that for sports…that place was buzzing."

she walks up to me and says, 'Hey Rivers, thought you wouldn't be here, didn't you?'"

Taking a cue from their superstar, Celtics fans were a confident bunch. After Game 6, Larry Bird had said, "They might as well forget it, they've got no chance… They had a chance to beat us and we all knew if we lost it meant vacation tomorrow." Bird's guarantee might have intimidated your average player, but in this case, his words lit a fire under the last person on earth he wanted to provoke. In Game 7 of the 1988 Eastern Conference Semifinals, the "Human Highlight Film" put on a show that will never be forgotten.

Mindful of Dominique's explosive speed, Bird gives him plenty of room.

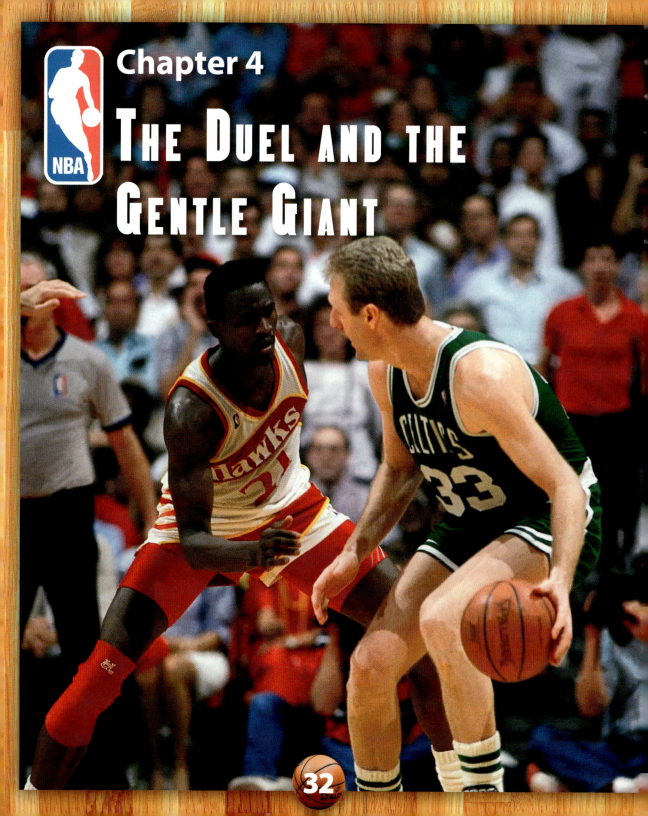

Chapter 4
The Duel and the Gentle Giant

Game 7 is not only remembered as one of the greatest playoff games of all time, it is considered to be one of the best games ever played, period. While the entire game was played at a high level, Dominique Wilkins and Larry Bird's fourth quarter performances inspired the name "The Duel" and made the game the stuff of legend.

Entering the fourth quarter, the Celtics held a two-point lead. Dominique led all scorers with 31 points, while players like Kevin McHale, Doc Rivers, and Kevin Whitman were not far behind. But when the buzzer sounded, marking the beginning of the fourth quarter, it was as if the bell had been rung for the last round of a championship fight. The two heavyweights, Bird and Dominique, stepped into the ring and started throwing haymakers.

Dominique recalled Kevin Willis, pointing at Bird and saying to him, "Don't let that son of a gun score anymore, man." Dominique thought to himself, "What are you doing?" According to Dominique, Bird's eyes

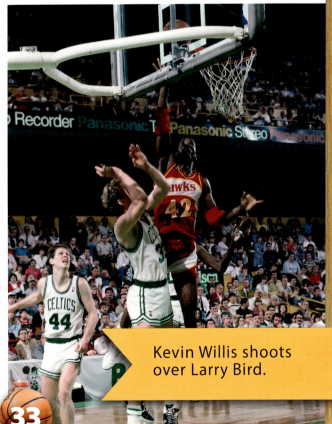

Kevin Willis shoots over Larry Bird.

got huge and Dominique, "knew it was going to be on then." Bird drained a jumper and the shootout began.

Throughout the fourth quarter, Bird and Dominique matched each other shot for shot. These shots did not include any breakaway dunks or lay-ups. In fact, because neither team was missing or turning the ball over, there were almost zero fast break opportunities in the quarter. Every time down the court, the other team's defense was set, and every play they ran was simple: get Bird or Dominique the ball and get out of their way. Bird and Dominique hit an array of jump shots from all kinds of angles. They forced their way into clogged lanes to make seemingly impossible six to eight-foot shots over the outstretched hands of seven-foot defenders.

In the fourth quarter known as "The Duel," Larry Bird hit nine of 10 shots, scoring 20 points. Dominique made eight baskets of his own, scoring 16 of his playoff career-high 47. Each shot was more incredible than the last. According

Bird shoots over Dominique.

to Doc Rivers, some of the shots weren't the kind you'd normally want your teammate to take. "I don't think either one of them took easy shots. You could categorize half their makes as bad shots that went in… It got to the point they were looking for those shots… and making them all." When players get that hot, normal basketball strategy no longer applies. Bird and Dominique might as well have been the only two players on the court. And the question that decided that game was not who would miss first, but who would get the ball last.

When the dust finally settled and the final buzzer sounded, the Celtics had won. They eked out a 118-116 win and moved onto the next round. As the players were walking off the floor, Bird said to Dominique: "We both deserved to win… unfortunately somebody has to go home."

By the start of the next season,

Empty Stomachs
According to Rivers, none of the Hawks players received room service in their hotel before the game. It was rumored that Celtics' owner Red Aeurbach was behind the poor service.

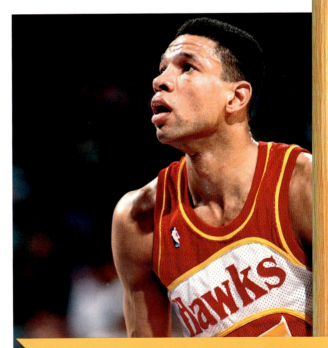

While 'Nique scorched the nets, Doc dished out 18 assists to go along with his 16 points.

Moses Malone stands beside Hakeem Olajuwon, Michael Jordan, and Magic Johnson at the 1988 All-Star Game.

trades had changed the face of the Hawks. In an effort to provide Dominique some offensive help, management traded Tree Rollins and Randy Wittman and acquired Reggie Theus and Hall of Fame center, Moses Malone. On paper, the moves looked good. Unfortunately, the team didn't perform the way management had hoped. They never quite reached the level of play they had in 1988. Despite big numbers from Dominique Wilkins, the Hawks couldn't make it out of the first-round of the playoffs. Then, during the 1993-94 season, the "Human Highlight Film" was traded to the Los Angeles Clippers. His 23,292 points in a Hawks uniform remain the most in the team's history.

The reshaping of the Hawks

Down to Earth
After leaving the Hawks, 'Nique played for six teams (two overseas) before retiring in 1999.

took many different forms. From 1993 to the year 2000, former St. Louis Hawks guard Lenny Wilkins coached the team to six straight playoff appearances. A nine-time All-Star, Wilkins coached the Seattle SuperSonics to the team's only NBA championship in 1979. He kept on winning from there. In fact, while coaching the Hawks, Wilkins became the winningest coach of all time, passing the Celtics' legendary skipper, Red Auerbach. In 1994, Wilkins was named Coach of the Year and guided a team led by Danny Manning, Stacey Augmon, Mookie Blaylock, and Kevin Willis to the Central Division title. This team was much improved on the defensive end, but without Dominique, they struggled to score in the playoffs,

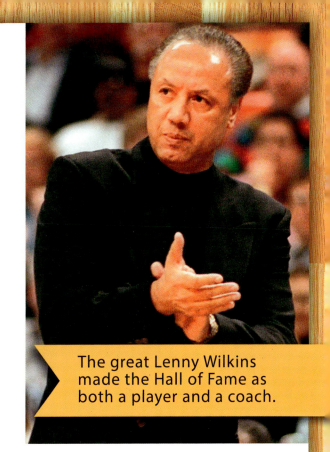

The great Lenny Wilkins made the Hall of Fame as both a player and a coach.

losing to the Indiana Pacers in the second round.

A big man with an even bigger smile anchored the strongest Hawks' teams of the late 1990s. With shooting guard Steve Smith leading the team in scoring, Dikembe Mutombo, the 7'2" center from the Democratic Republic of the Congo

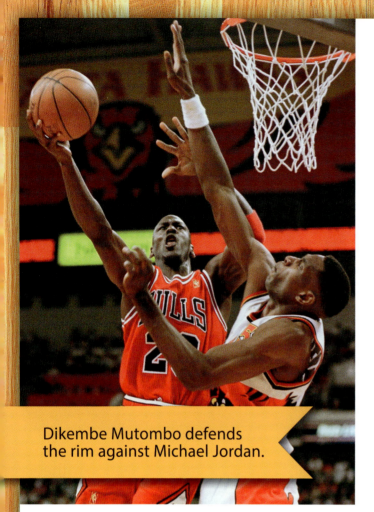

Dikembe Mutombo defends the rim against Michael Jordan.

2.9 and 3.4 blocks per game. In addition to the numbers, he earned some impressive hardware, capturing back-to-back Defensive Player of the Year awards in 1997 and 1998. Mutombo's famous finger-wag in the faces of players whose shots he had just blocked made him a villain to his opponents. But there was no questioning Mutombo's giant heart. The Hawks' big man was one of the greatest philanthropists in the history of the NBA.

in Africa, became perhaps the most intimidating defensive presence to ever wear a Hawks uniform. The perfect player for Lenny Wilkins' defense-first coaching style, Mutombo became a star in Atlanta. For four years he averaged between

In 1997, Mutombo started the Dikembe Mutombo Foundation to improve living conditions in the Democratic Republic of Congo. In addition to this, he donated $15 million of his own money to build a hospital in the Congolese capital of Kinshasa. When asked about his generosity, Mutombo said, "For me, the real reward will be the day I walk into this new building and see people receiving the vital care that they need." Mutombo's commitment to his community reminded sports fans of athletes like Muhammad Ali and the great Puerto Rican baseball player, Roberto Clemente. These were men who had made incredible sacrifices to help improve the lives of their people. Like Ali and Clemente, Mutombo recognized the influence his status as a sports star gave him, and he didn't hesitate to use it to benefit others.

"There is a proverb in Africa,"

Model Citizen
Mutombo has twice won the J. Walter Kennedy Citizenship Award, given annually to a player, coach, or trainer who shows "outstanding service and dedication to the community."

says Mutombo. "When you take the elevator to go up, you always must remember to send it back down. This is my way of sending it back down."

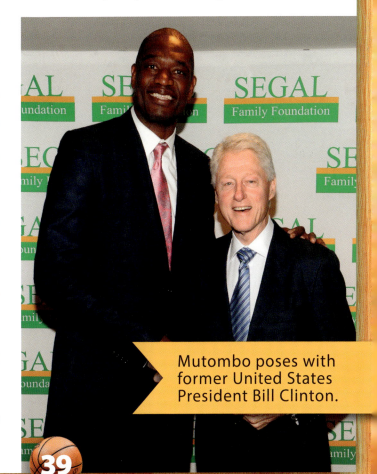

Mutombo poses with former United States President Bill Clinton.

Chapter 5
Soaring into the Future

Starting with Mutombo's final year in a Hawks' uniform, the team labored through an eight-year playoff drought. Other than the opening of the ultra-modern Philips Arena, there was little to be excited about in Atlanta. During this period, the Hawks welcomed back Dominique Wilkins, announcing him as the team's Vice President of Basketball Operations. For Hawks fans, it felt good to see the Human Highlight Film on the sidelines. The man who had injected so much excitement into Atlanta basketball, who had created an atmosphere of electricity in the Omni every night he suited up, had come home. And while they might never again get to see him lace up his shoes and rise high above the rim for a thunderous jam, fans were heartened by his presence in the building. Then came the 2005 Slam Dunk competition, and all of sudden it looked as though Dominique had been reborn.

While the 2004-05 season was

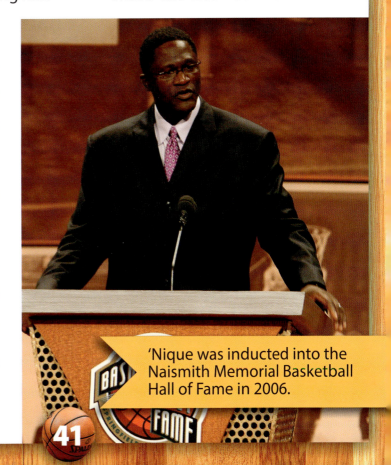

'Nique was inducted into the Naismith Memorial Basketball Hall of Fame in 2006.

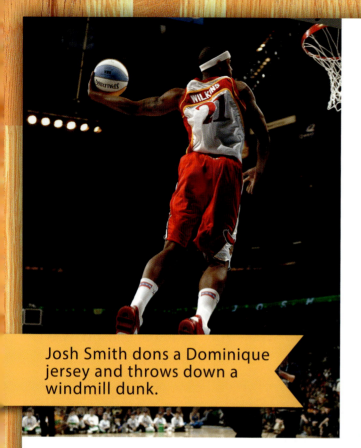

Josh Smith dons a Dominique jersey and throws down a windmill dunk.

not one that Hawks fans remember fondly, rookie Josh Smith registered a performance for the ages, during the NBA's All-Star weekend. Dominique Wilkins began his career in 1982, three years before Josh Smith was born. But despite his youth, no one needed to lecture Josh about the legacy of Hawk domination at this event. With Dominique Wilkins watching from his courtside seat, Smith honored his predecessor and delighted the crowd by changing into a number 21 Wilkins jersey for one of his final dunks. He then slammed home a vicious windmill, sending the crowd into a frenzy and earning himself a perfect score. Smith won the competition and kindled Hawks fans' hopes for a thrilling future.

By the 2007-08 season, the future seemed to have arrived. The Hawks added swingman Joe Johnson and two-time NCAA champion Al Horford. Johnson's ability to create

Dynamic Dunkers
Josh Smith was the first Hawk to win the dunk contest since Dominique won his second title in 1990.

his own shot, score at a high percentage, and find the open teammate, made him one of the league's premiere offensive players. And at 6'10" and 250 pounds, young Al Horford was an inside scoring threat and a beast on the boards. Unfortunately for the Hawks, injuries prevented the team from being a consistent winner. While the team showed flashes of brilliance, they limped into the playoffs eight games below .500 for a series with their old nemesis—the Boston Celtics. After being soundly beaten in Games 1 and 2, few expected the Hawks to win a single game against Boston's Big Three of Kevin Garnett, Paul Pierce, and Ray Allen. Then something changed.

The Hawks came home to Atlanta

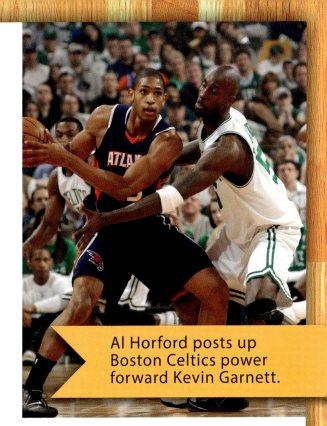

Al Horford posts up Boston Celtics power forward Kevin Garnett.

and won Game 3. The Celtics hadn't played poorly; they had simply been outplayed. The Hawks shared the ball incredibly well, assisting on 28 of the team's 36 baskets. Smith and Johnson hit a barrage of threes and rookie Horford scored 17 to go along with his 14 rebounds. But like most games, the numbers only told part of the story. The real story of that game was an energized Atlanta crowd. With Dominique Wilkins leading the cheers, Hawks fans were as loud and raucous as they had been in the 1988 playoffs. They recognized that their team was better than their record. They could plainly see that the Hawks' athleticism presented problems for the older Celtics. Suddenly the first-round series had all the drama and emotion of a Conference Finals match-up.

Despite losing lopsided games in Boston, the Hawks beat the Celtics three times in Atlanta. Energized by the wild Philips Arena crowd, their confidence grew game by game, so that by the end of Game 6, most NBA fans were scratching their heads, wondering how it was that this team had been a #8 seed. They were just too good.

The truth was, they *were* too good. And while the Hawks ended up losing to the Celtics in seven games, the next season proved that they were now among the Eastern Conference's elite teams.

In the 2008-09 season, the Hawks rose to 2nd place in the Southwest Division. They also won

Joe Johnson launches a deep jumper over Rajon Rondo.

their first playoff series since 1999. Unfortunately, they weren't quite ready for LeBron James's Cleveland Cavaliers and they were swept out of the playoffs. The next year followed the same pattern: the Hawks played very well, won over 50 games for the first time in 10 years, beat their first-round opponent, but were swept out of the playoffs by Dwight Howard's Orlando Magic. Something was wrong. When would one of their young stars emerge as a leader and instill in these Hawks the confidence to stand up to the Eastern Conference's best teams?

Entering the 2013-14 season, one thing Hawks' fans know is that their team will have an array of talented players. While the Hawks lost Josh Smith to free agency, they were able to sign rock-steady power forward Paul Millsap to a two-year deal. After becoming a starter in Utah in 2010, Millsap averaged between 14.6 and 17.3 points, and 7.1 and 8.8 rebounds per game. A quiet but steady presence on the floor, Millsap leads by example.

Joining Millsap in the paint will be a dominant power forward/center in Al Horford. Coming off a career year in which he averaged 17.4 points and 10.2 rebounds per game, outstanding play from the man in the middle is a given. Together, Horford and Millsap will comprise a 500-pound duo controlling the paint.

Beast on the Boards
While attending Louisiana Tech University, Paul Millsap became the only player in NCAA basketball history to lead the nation in rebounding for three consecutive years.

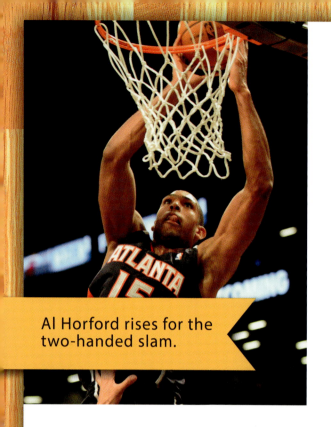

Al Horford rises for the two-handed slam.

In Jeff Teague, the Hawks have the kind of outstanding young point guard they sorely lacked in 2008 through 2010. With great speed and a knack for getting to the rim, Teague can score and create loads of opportunities for his teammates. In the 2013 offseason, the Hawks inked Teague to a four-year deal, ensuring that the Hawks floor general will continue to grow in Atlanta. Coming off a season in which he averaged career highs in points (14.6) and assists (7.2), the sky is the limit.

With Teague's ability to collapse the defense and get into the lane, Hawks shooters should have plenty of open looks. In Louis Williams and Kyle Korver, the Hawks have two of the league's premiere three-point threats.

In the 2013-14 season, head coach Mike Budenholzer will bring his championship pedigree to the Atlanta Hawks. Budenholzer spent 16 years on the sidelines as an assistant to Gregg Popovich in San Antonio, where the Spurs were models of consistency, sharing the ball on offense, playing great team defense, and winning multiple titles.

Working alongside the new head coach is another former Spurs employee, General Manager Danny Ferry. Among other duties, Ferry will be trying to free up salary cap space for 2014, when a bonanza of talented players such as LeBron James, Carmelo Anthony, Dwyane Wade, and Kobe Bryant will decide whether or not they'd like to try out a new city. Having found his coach, Ferry will have to decide which of these tremendous athletes are best suited for the team, and pursue those players with the same tenacity that the Hawks will use to pursue a division title.

Whatever the future holds, there's no time like the present. In the 2013-14 season, Hawks fans

Jeff Teague soars above three Miami Heat defenders.

Postseason Players

In the 2013-14 season, the Hawks will attempt to make the playoffs for the seventh straight year.

hope that a core trio of Horford, Millsap, and Teague will thrive under Budenholzer's system. They hope to see their Hawks play with the passion and skill of the Dominique-led teams from the 1980s, and with the determination that propelled Bob Petit's Hawks to a title in 1958.

Atlanta sports icons like "Hammerin" Hank Aaron and Dominique Wilkins know firsthand the way their city gets behind athletes who leave it all on the court. The time has come for this new generation of Hawks to feed off their fans, and play with the confidence generated by having an entire city behind them. The Hawks franchise traveled a great distance before finding a home in Atlanta. For many years, it was good enough that they competed. But the time for raised expectations has arrived, for the newest generation of Hawks to take flight and soar atop the Eastern Conference.

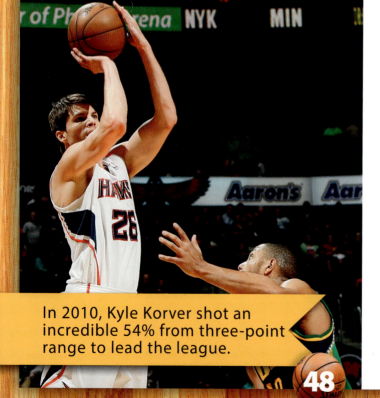

In 2010, Kyle Korver shot an incredible 54% from three-point range to lead the league.